For you, Tegan Chloë Rose . . .

OXFORD
UNIVERSITY PRESS

Great Clarendon Street, Oxford OX2 6DP

Oxford University Press is a department of the University of Oxford.
It furthers the University's objective of excellence in research, scholarship,
and education by publishing worldwide in

Oxford New York

Auckland Cape Town Dar es Salaam Hong Kong Karachi
Kuala Lumpur Madrid Melbourne Mexico City Nairobi
New Delhi Shanghai Taipei Toronto

With offices in
Argentina Austria Brazil Chile Czech Republic France Greece
Guatemala Hungary Italy Japan Poland Portugal Singapore
South Korea Switzerland Thailand Turkey Ukraine Vietnam

Text & Illustration copyright © Layn Marlow

The moral rights of the author and artist have been asserted

Database right Oxford University Press (maker)

First published 2013

British Library Cataloguing in Publication Data available

ISBN: 978-0-19-279473-4 (hardback)

10 9 8 7 6 5 4 3 2 1

Printed in China

Paper used in the production of this book is a natural, recyclable product made
from wood grown in sustainable forests. The manufacturing process conforms
to the environmental regulations of the country of origin

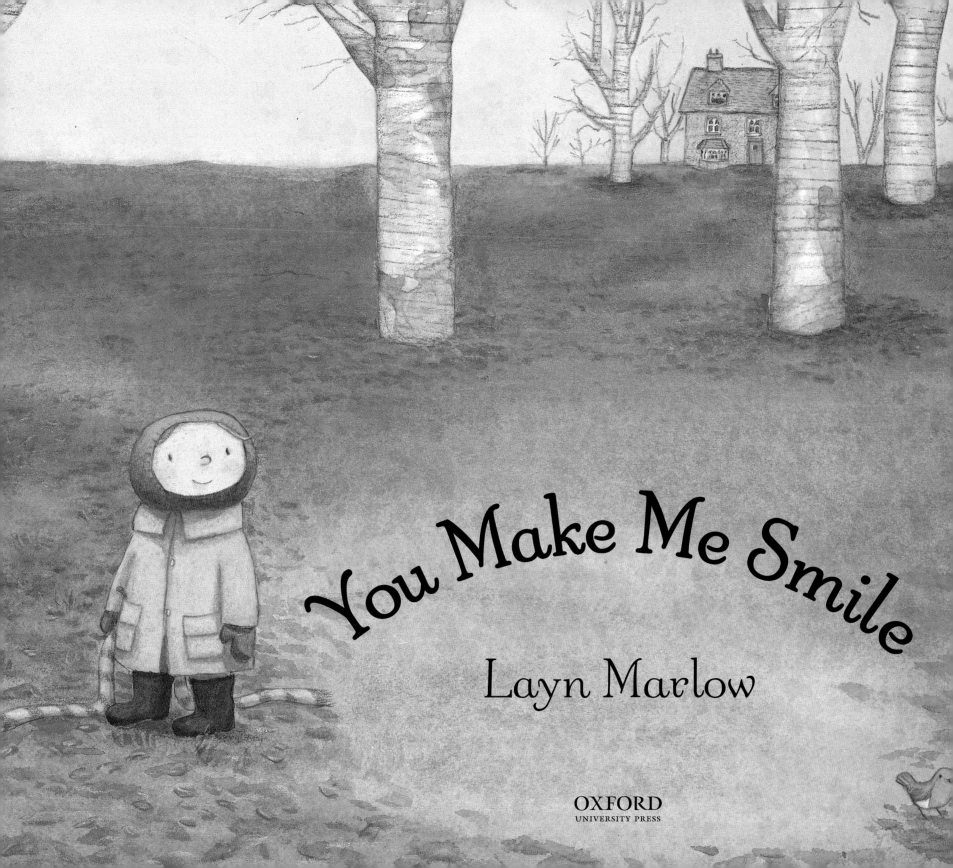

You Make Me Smile

Layn Marlow

OXFORD
UNIVERSITY PRESS

Of all the days in all the seasons
of the year, today is a very special day.

You might not think so yet,
but it really is!

The day starts wintry grey.

But look!

Suddenly, silently
frozen flakes are falling
from the sky.

And ever so softly
all around, snow, snow,
snow is covering
the ground!

Hooray!

Soon you'll be standing outside . . .

in the bright, white world.

You'll be cold,

cold,

cold,

with a radish-red nose.

Your arms may be stiff,
but your eyes
are going to shine.

A long woollen scarf
around your neck
should keep you warm,

but the cold
doesn't seem to
matter to you,

because . . .

today is the special day . . .

when

you

make

me . . .

smile.

'Smile!'

Tomorrow may be warmer.
Winter turns to spring.
A year may pass,
    but if you wait . . .

. . . we can share a snowy smile again.